First Library of Knowledge

Dinosaurs

and Other Prehistoric Life

BLACKBIRCH PRESS

An imprint of Thomson Gale, a part of The Thomson Corporation

Detroit • New York • San Francisco • San Diego • New Haven, Conn. • Waterville, Maine • London • Munich

First published in 2005 by Orpheus Books Ltd., 2 Church Green, Witney, Oxfordshire, OX28 4AW

First published in North America in 2006 by Thomson Gale

Copyright © 2005 Orpheus Books Ltd.

Created and produced: Rachel Coombs, Nicholas Harris, Sarah Harrison, Sarah Hartley, Emma Helbrough, Orpheus Books Ltd.

Text: Nicholas Harris

Consultant: Professor Michael Benton, Department of Geology, Bristol University

Illustrators: Inklink Firenze, Nicki Palin, Gary Hincks, Peter Dennis

For more information, contact
Blackbirch Press
27500 Drake Rd.
Farmington Hills, MI 48331-3535
Or you can visit our Internet site at http://www.gale.com

LIBRARY OF CONGRESS CATALOGING-IN-PUBLICATIONS

Harris, Nicholas.
Dinosaurs and other prehistoric life / by Nicholas Harris.
p. cm. -- (First library of knowledge)
Includes glossary and index.
ISBN 1-4103-0350-0 (hardcover : alk. paper)
1. Dinosaurs--Encyclopedias, Juvenile. [1. Dinosaurs—Encyclopedias.
2. TITLE.] I. Title. II. Series.
CIP Record Information for this title available from the Library of Congress CIP Division

Printed in Malaysia
10 9 8 7 6 5 4 3 2 1

CONTENTS

INTRODUCTION

EARTH is about 4.6 billion years old. Life on our planet probably began about 3.8 billion years ago. The first life-forms were **microscopic** things, neither animals nor plants. It was another 3.6 billion years before a certain kind of **reptile** appeared. Some of these reptiles were the largest and fiercest creatures that ever lived. They were the dinosaurs.

HOW THE EARTH BEGAN

The fragments collected in orbit around the Earth, which was by now a ball of melted rock (3).

The Earth's surface later cooled and turned back to solid rock. The orbiting fragments came together to form the Moon (4).

1

Soon after the Earth formed, another small planet (1) collided with it and exploded (2).

2

3

LIKE all the planets, the Earth was formed about 4.6 billion years ago. In its early years, it had no water or life, just **barren** rock. Meteorites (large boulders), rained down from space. Life probably arose 3.8 billion years ago.

THE SOLAR SYSTEM

The planets were once billions of small rocks whirling round the Sun. They snowballed into large, rocky globes.

At first, the Earth was a barren planet. But volcanoes blasted out gases from beneath its surface. One of these gases was water vapor. Clouds formed (5) and, later, rain fell. It rained for millions of years until basins filled to become the oceans (6).

All forms of life need water to survive. Life may have arisen in the Earth's warm, shallow seas.

THE FIRST LIVING THINGS

THE FIRST living things appeared not on land, but in the oceans. They were very tiny life- forms called bacteria. The first animals were soft- bodied sea creatures, such as jellyfish and worms.

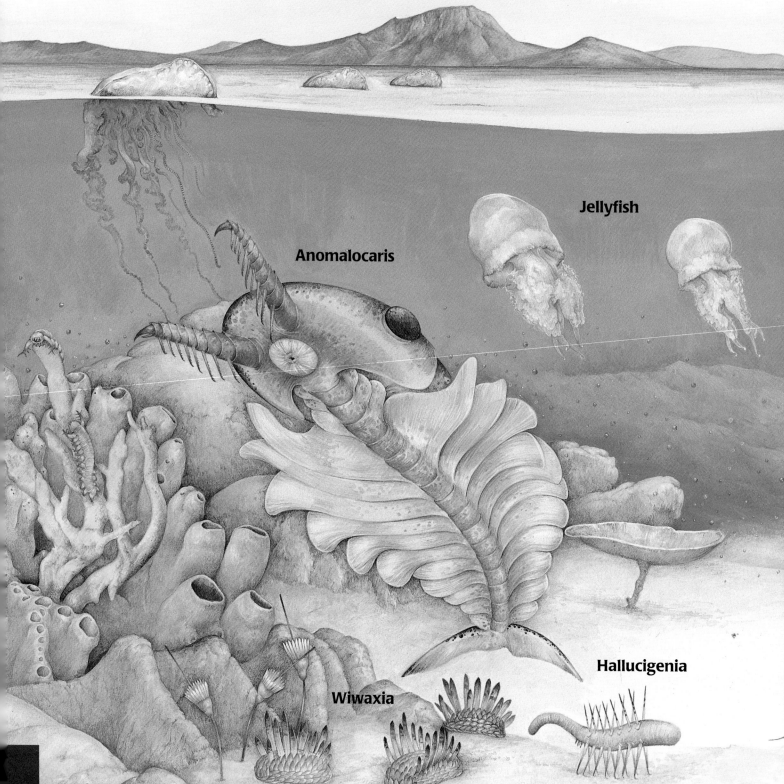

Jellyfish

Anomalocaris

Wiwaxia

Hallucigenia

THE CAMBRIAN SEAS

The first animals with hard parts—shells or bony skeletons—first appeared about 540 million years ago. This was at the beginning of a time in Earth's history that scientists call the Cambrian Period.

These animals lived in warm, shallow seas. They included shellfish, corals, starfish, mollusks, and sponges. Some very strange-looking animals swam in the Cambrian seas! One, Opabinia, had five mushroom-shaped eyes.

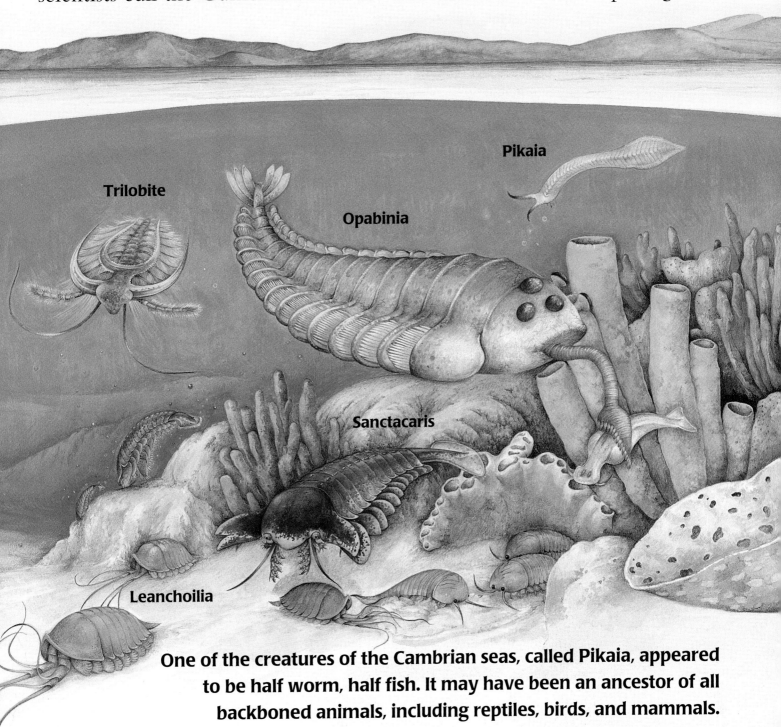

One of the creatures of the Cambrian seas, called Pikaia, appeared to be half worm, half fish. It may have been an ancestor of all backboned animals, including reptiles, birds, and mammals.

THE FIRST FISH

Water scorpions were fierce animals. They scuttled around on the sea floor hunting fish. They caught prey in their claws.

THE FIRST fish had no fins or jaws. They swam with their mouths open, sucking in things to eat.

A trilobite used its legs to walk on the seafloor, or to paddle through the water.

The first fish had bony armor plating to defend them from attack.

TRILOBITES

Trilobites first appeared in the Cambrian seas. They were very common for the next 250 million years. Their bodies were divided into three lengthwise strips, or lobes. They used their legs to carry food to their mouths. Some kinds could roll themselves into a ball for protection.

FISH WITH JAWS

Over millions of years, fish with fins appeared. Fins allowed them to steer more easily and swim faster. Some fish also had jaws and teeth. They were able to feed on other sea creatures.

Dunkleosteus was a 30-foot-long (9 meters) sea monster. Instead of teeth it had huge plates of bone in its jaws. These sliced like razor blades.

COAL SWAMPS

ABOUT 350 million years ago, some parts of the world were covered by hot, steamy jungles. Giant dragonflies flitted among the trees. Huge centipedes and **amphibians** lurked in the swampy undergrowth. The coal we have today was formed from peat, a dark soil that was produced from layers of rotting plant matter in these swamps.

Dendrerpeton
(ancient amphibian)

AMPHIBIANS

Some kinds of fish, called lobefins, had fleshy fins that they used to heave themselves onto land. Eventually, they spent most their lives on land, returning to the water only to lay eggs. They were the first amphibians.

Hylonomus (ancient reptile)

Giant centipede

Giant dragonfly

THE FIRST DINOSAURS

SOME amphibians became able to lay their eggs on land, avoiding the need to return to water. Since they could live on dry lands, these animals, the first reptiles, spread all over the world. Some kinds of reptiles could run about on two legs. They were the first dinosaurs.

A modern reptile (above) has legs at the side of its body. A dinosaur (right) had straight, upright legs.

WHAT IS A DINOSAUR?

Dinosaurs were reptiles that lived on land in the Triassic, Jurassic, and Cretaceous periods (250-65 million years ago). They walked upright like mammals or birds, not sprawling like other reptiles. Neither marine reptiles nor flying reptiles (pterosaurs) were dinosaurs.

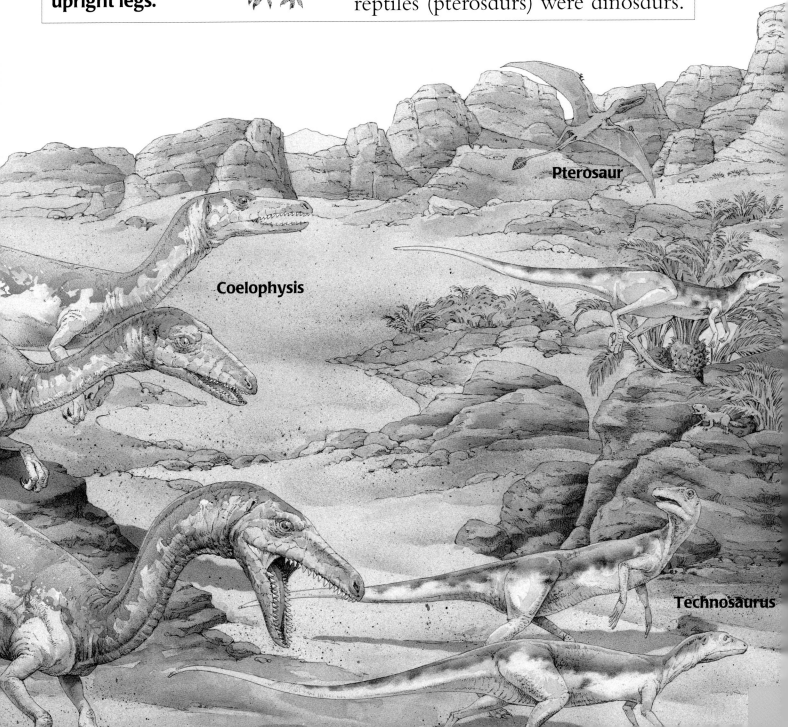

Pterosaur

Coelophysis

Technosaurus

JURASSIC DINOSAURS

THE first dinosaurs were flesh eaters. But by the Jurassic Period there were also many plant-eating kinds. These included the long-necked sauropods and the stegosaurs, dinosaurs with plates running down their backs. The 40-foot-long (12 meters) Allosaurus preyed on these plant eaters.

Ornitholestes

THE FIRST BIRDS

The first birds appeared in the Jurassic Period. They were probably descended from small flesh-eating dinosaurs. Some of these dinosaurs are known to have had feathers.

Archaeopteryx

Diplodocus (long-necked sauropod)

Stegosaurus

Allosaurus

Allosaurus

Camarasaurus

PLANT-EATING DINOSAURS

Brachiosaurus was a giant plant-eating sauropod taller than a four-story building. Its sheer size protected it from attack. Tiny Hypsilophodon lived in herds. It sprinted for safety whenever threatened.

Brachiosaurus

Acrocanthosaurus

Iguanodon

FIGHTING BACK

No plant-eating dinosaur could afford to be off its guard. A flesh eater might launch an attack at any time. An Iguanodon was not large enough to fight an attacker off or quick enough to run away. Instead, it had sharp spikes for thumbs. If any dinosaur dared to attack it, the Iguanodon would rear up on its back legs and jab a spike into the **predator's** body.

MARINE REPTILES

Reptiles were also masters of the oceans. Ichthyosaurs looked like dolphins, while plesiosaurs, with their small heads and long necks, resembled dinosaurs.

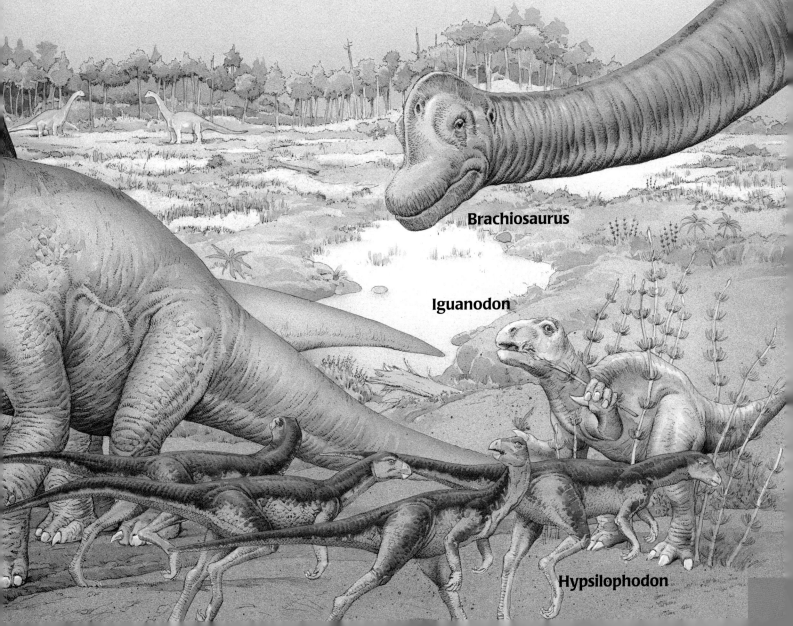

Brachiosaurus

Iguanodon

Hypsilophodon

FLESH-EATING DINOSAURS

SOME plant-eating dinosaurs had a covering of bony armor to protect them from attack. Sauropelta was covered in studs and spikes. But a gang of Deinonychus knew how to overcome its defenses. They had a massive, curved claw on each foot. Rushing at their prey,

Deinonychus

Sauropelta

they used these claws to slash through the hide, fatally wounding their victim.

DINOSAUR PREDATORS

The flesh-eating dinosaurs, known as theropods, all moved about on two legs. These kept their front limbs free for grasping their prey. Large theropods hunted alone, while some smaller ones worked together in packs.

Deinonychus

DUCK-BILLED DINOSAURS

THESE dinosaurs lived in the Cretaceous Period. Their snouts were wide and flat, and looked like duck's bills. They had hundreds of long-wearing teeth in their jaws. This allowed them to feed on all kinds of plants, including leaves, ferns, and pine needles.

Edmontosaurus

Parasaurolophus

HOLLOW CRESTS

Many duckbills had crests on top of their heads. Parasaurolophus had a very long, backward-pointing one. These crests were hollow with tubes inside, and were connected to the nose and throat.

They probably helped make the dinosaur's warning calls to other members of its herd much louder and deeper.

Pteranodon

Corythosaurus

Lambeosaurus

CRETACEOUS DINOSAURS

TWO of the best-known dinosaurs lived at the end of the Cretaceous Period. The plant eater, Triceratops, had three horns on its head and a large neck frill. Tyrannosaurus rex was one of the few predators powerful enough to attack it.

Triceratops

Triceratops

The first mammals appeared in the Age of Dinosaurs. They were tiny creatures, that usually emerged only at night to feed.

Ancient mammal

While dinosaurs ruled on land, pterosaurs such as Pteranodon flew in the skies. Sheets of skin between the fourth finger and body made up their wings. They used their beaks for seizing fish.

Pteranodon

Tyrannosaurus rex

KING OF DINOSAURS

One of the largest flesh-eating dinosaurs, 40-foot-long (12 meters) Tyrannosaurus rex had huge, powerful legs and teeth as sharp as steak knives. It would charge at its prey, bringing it down with the huge claws on its feet.

THE END OF THE DINOSAURS

AT THE END of the Cretaceous Period, all the dinosaurs suddenly died out. No one knows why this happened. It was not only dinosaurs that became **extinct**. Pterosaurs and many kinds of sea creatures also disappeared forever. The world may have become a bleak, cold desert for a time, where only a few kinds of animals could survive.

Tyrannosaurus re

WHY DID THE DINOSAURS BECOME EXTINCT?

Many scientists think that a giant asteroid (a rocky object in space) crashed to Earth at this time. Millions of tons of rock and dust would have been thrown high into the sky by the explosion. This would have blotted out the Sun and changed the weather for years. The Earth would have become a frozen world.

PREHISTORIC BIRDS AND MAMMALS

BIRDS and mammals survived when the dinosaurs were wiped out. Prehistoric kinds were very different from modern ones.

Diatryma, a flightless bird, lived 60 million years ago.

Hyracotherium
(a prehistoric horse)

GIANT BIRDS

When Tyrannosaurus became extinct, there were no giant predators—for a while. Then, massive, flightless birds, 10 feet (3 meters) tall, took their place. These fierce, fast-running beasts preyed on small horses, crushing them to death in their huge, pointed beaks.

THE STORY OF MAMMALS

While the dinosaurs lived, mammals were tiny, shrew-like creatures. When dinosaurs disappeared, many kinds of mammals evolved (changed over time). They included the ancestors of horses, elephants, cats, whales, bats, monkeys—and humans.

Chriacus (a prehistoric mammal)

Diatryma

THE FIRST HUMANS

THE FIRST human-like creatures lived in Africa, probably more than 4 million years ago. They were descended from apelike creatures, but unlike apes, they walked upright on two legs. Later, humans spread to all parts of the world.

The first tools used by humans were stone blades. They were made by striking one stone against another to make a sharp edge.

APE-MEN

Early humans lived together in small groups. They were still apelike in appearance. About 2.5 million years ago, these humans were able to make simple stone tools. They used them to kill and skin animals.

NEANDERTHALS

Neanderthal humans evolved about 400,000 years ago. They were named after the valley in Germany where their bones were first discovered. Short and stocky, they had low foreheads, thick ridges above their eyes, and wide noses. They hunted and fished, cooked their food over fires, built shelters, and buried their dead. They lived until about 30,000 years ago.

Wooly mammoth caught in trap

Neanderthal hunters

DINOSAUR FOSSILS

DINOSAURS may have died out 65 million years ago, but the search goes on today for their fossils (their remains, turned to stone). Scientists can find out all about dinosaurs—what they ate, how fast they ran, how smart they were—from studying their fossils.

They look for fossils in rocks that were formed during the Age of Dinosaurs. Besides bones, they may also find footprints or eggs.

EXCAVATION SITE

The fossil hunters use picks and shovels to clear the rock away. They use blades or toothbrushes to do careful work. After recording the exact size and position of their finds, they pack the bones in foam or plaster and take them away.

HOW FOSSILS FORM

Fossils form when a dead animal is buried in sediments (sand or mud). Its soft parts rot away. Chemicals in water fill the tiny spaces inside the hard parts such as bone, teeth, or shell. Over millions of years, the sediments turn to stone, leaving the shape of the animal as a fossil.

GLOSSARY

amphibians: Animals that can live both on land and in water.

barren: Empty and lifeless.

extinct: When no members of a species remain alive.

microscopic: Something so small that it can only be seen through a microscope.

predator: An animal that hunts and kills other animals for food.

reptile: A cold-blooded, usually egg-laying animal such as a lizard or turtle.

INDEX